STERLING and the distinctive Sterling logo
are registered trademarks of Sterling Publishing Co., Inc.

**Library of Congress Cataloging-in-Publication Data**

Mayer, Mercer, 1943-
Little Critter's the night before Christmas / by Mercer Mayer.
p. cm.
"Based on The Night Before Christmas by Clement C. Moore"--copyright
p.
ISBN 978-1-4027-6799-9
1.  Santa Claus--Juvenile poetry. 2.  Christmas--Juvenile poetry. 3.
Children's poetry, American.  I. Moore, Clement Clarke, 1779-1863. Night
before Christmas. II. Title.
PS3563.A9527L58 2009
811'.54--dc22
2009015866

2  4  6  8  10  9  7  5  3  1
07/10

Originally published in the U.S. by B. Dalton Booksellers, Inc.,
a division of Barnes and Noble Bookstores, Inc.
Copyright ©1992 by Mercer Mayer.

Based on "The Night Before Christmas" by Clement C. Moore.

Published by Sterling Publishing Co., Inc.
387 Park Avenue South, New York, NY 10016
Distributed in Canada by Sterling Publishing
c/o Canadian Manda Group, 165 Dufferin Street
Toronto, Ontario, Canada M6K 3H6

A Big Tuna New Media LLC/ J.R. Sansevere Book

*Printed in China*
*All rights reserved.*

Sterling ISBN 978-1-4027-6799-9

For information about custom editions, special sales, premium
and corporate purchases, please contact Sterling Special Sales
Department at 800-805-5489 or specialsales@sterlingpublishing.com.

# LITTLE CRITTER'S
# THE NIGHT BEFORE
# CHRISTMAS

## BY
## MERCER MAYER

STERLING

New York / London

'Twas the night before Christmas when all through the house,
Not a critter was stirring, not even a mouse.

The stockings were hung by the chimney with care,
In hopes that Santa Claus soon would be there.

We were nestled all snug in our beds,
While visions of sugarplums danced in our heads.

And Mom in her kerchief, and Dad in his cap,

Had just settled down for a long winter's nap,

When out on the lawn there arose such a clatter,
I sprang from my bed to see what was the matter.

Away to the window I flew like a flash,
Tore open the shutters and threw up the sash.

When what to my wondering eyes should appear
But an old-fashioned sleigh with eight prancing reindeer.
With a little old driver so lively and quick,
I knew in a moment it must be St. Nick.

More rapid than eagles his reindeer they came,
And he whistled and shouted and called them by name:
"Now, Dasher! Now, Dancer! Now, Prancer and Vixen!
On, Comet! On, Cupid! On, Donder and Blitzen!"

So up to the housetop the reindeer flew,
With a sleigh full of toys and Santa Claus, too.

And then in a twinkle I heard on the roof
The prancing and pawing of each little hoof.
As I drew in my head and was turning around,
Down the chimney Santa Claus came with a bound.

He was dressed all in fur from his head to his foot,
And his clothes were all tarnished with ashes and soot.
A bundle of toys he had flung on his back,
And he looked like a peddler just opening his pack.

His eyes, how they twinkled! His dimples, how merry!

His cheeks were like roses, his nose like a cherry!

His comical mouth was drawn up like a bow,

And the beard on his chin was as white as the snow.

He had a broad face and a little round belly
That shook when he laughed like a bowl full of jelly.
He was chubby and plump, a right jolly old elf.
And I laughed when I saw him, in spite of myself.

He spoke not a word but went straight to his work,
And filled all the stockings, then turned with a jerk,
And laying his finger aside of his nose
And giving a nod, up the chimney he rose.

He sprang to his sleigh, to his team gave a whistle,
And away they all flew like the down of a thistle.
But I heard him exclaim as he drove out of sight: